FOR ZAC + RILEY !!

BOXES

WILL ROBERTSON

For those who counted
the cost and followed...

BOXES

WILL ROBERTSON

Once there was a boy,
and he had a box
and he would play in it
all day long.

Sometimes it was a castle,
or a spaceship,
or sometimes even a cave.

But it was always wonderful.

One day, the boy got a new coat, and he thought it was very special, so he put it into the box to keep it safe for winter.

But then the box wasn't as much fun to play in.

It was full of coats.

So the boy began to play next to the box, but that wasn't as entertaining, so he began to look for other things to do instead.

He bought a kite...

... and a big rubber ball
and some skis for when it was cold...

... and he put all of these
things into his box.

He did this for many years, and soon his box was completely filled with fun things to do.

But the boy was unhappy. He would spend long hours sitting in the grass, trying to remember all of the fun times he'd had with his box.

It made him sad to think about it.

One day, he saw a girl pushing her box across the grass and he asked her where she was going.

"I'm tired of it here," she said. "I have heard that there is a place where everyone is happy, and I am going there."

The boy thought that this was good news. He had always dreamed of somewhere like that, and so he wanted to go there as well.

He picked up all of his things and he piled them into his box and he began to push it in the direction he'd seen the girl go.

Sometimes the ground was smooth.
Sometimes it was bumpy...

... and sometimes there were hills...

... but he didn't mind because
he was so excited to be going to such
a wonderful place.

Finally, he came to where the land met the sea and he couldn't go any farther.

He saw a girl and he asked her if this was the place where everyone was happy. She shook her head in despair and pointed out across the water.

And the boy saw that there was an enormous crowd of children all around him as far as he could see. They had all pushed their own heavy boxes, piled high with things, and every one of them was looking sadly out at the sea, because there was no way for them to pass over.

And the boy stayed there for a long time, and the more he stared at the water, the more he knew there must be a way to cross it somehow.

He tried to jump across,
but his legs were too weak.

He tried to swim, but it was
too far and he had to be rescued.

And so he decided that it was hopeless. He threw himself down on the ground next to his box and a great pile of toys fell off the top and bounced off his head.

And he became angry and began to shout that he had been happier with just his box, before all of these things had filled it up and ruined it.

And as he said this, he began to pull them out of his box, one by one, and throw them into the sea until nothing was left.

He stood there for a moment, watching all of his things float away. Then he looked back at his empty box, lying lonely in the sand, and he began to remember all of the fun times that he'd had with his box when he was happy.

And he realized that what he wanted more than anything in the whole world was to have the chance to go on one more great adventure with his favorite box.

So he dragged his old friend down to the water and together, they set out on their grandest adventure yet.

And he was happy.

Made in the USA
San Bernardino, CA
29 October 2015